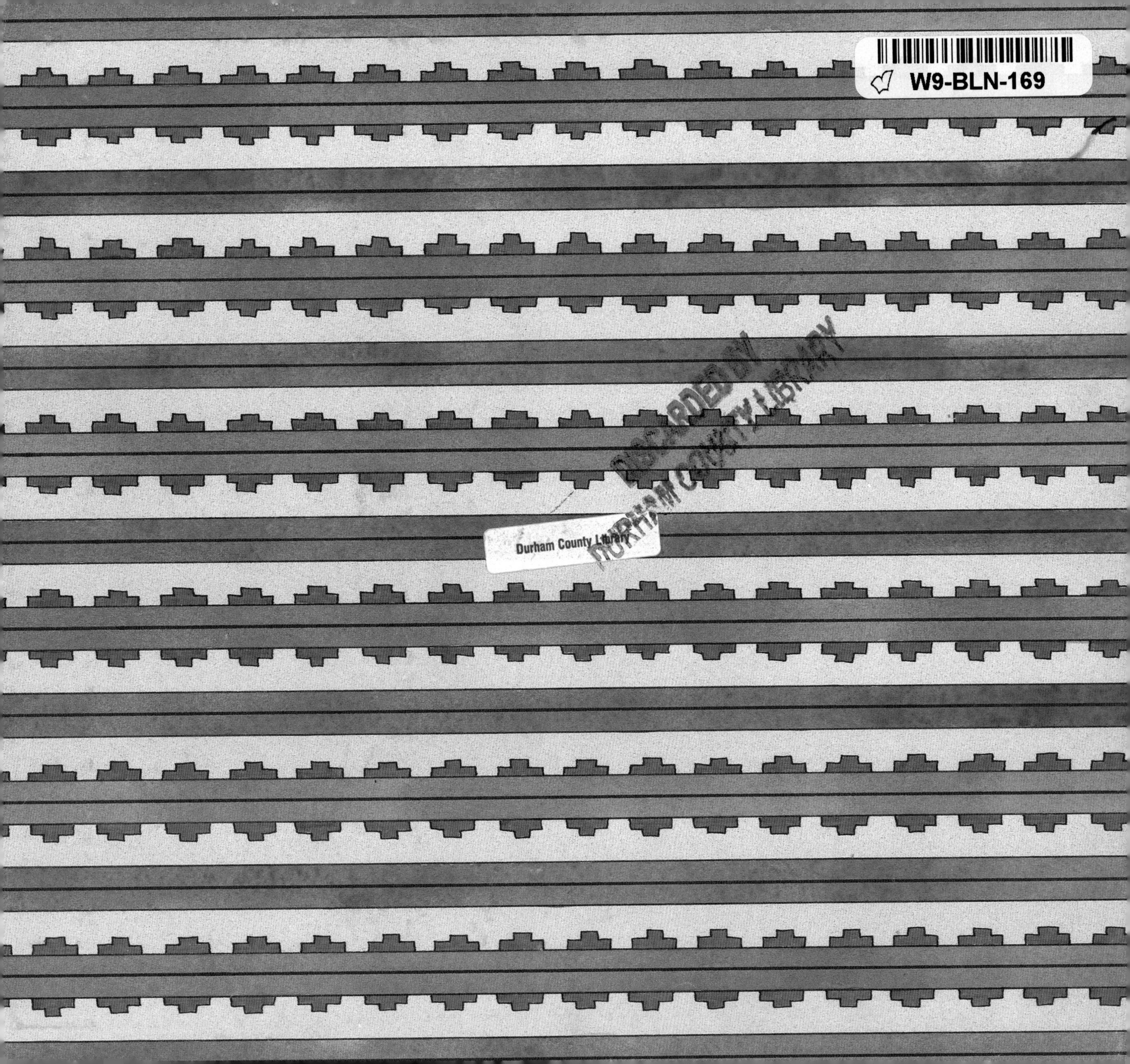
W9-BLN-169
Durham County Library
DISCARDED BY
DURHAM COUNTY LIBRARY

Book design by Julie Noyes.
Printed in Hong Kong.

Grossman, Virginia.
Ten little rabbits/by Virginia Grossman; illustrated by Syliva Long.
p. cm.
Summary: A counting rhyme with illustrations of rabbits in Native American costume, depicting traditional customs such as rain dances, hunting, and smoke signals. Includes a glossary with additional information on the customs.
ISBN 0-87701-552-X
1. Indians of North America–Social life and customs–Juvenile literature. 2. Counting-out rhymes–Juvenile literature. [1. Indians of North America–Social life and customs. 2. Counting.] I. Long, Sylvia, ill. II. Title.
E98.S7G87 1991
394'.08997–dc20
[E]
90-2011
CIP
AC

Distributed in Canada by Raincoast Books,
112 East Third Avenue, Vancouver, B.C. V5T 1C8

10 9 8 7 6 5 4 3

Chronicle Books
275 Fifth Street
San Francisco, California 94103

For Andrew, Emily, Gretchen, John, and Matthew

TEN LITTLE RABBITS

by Virginia Grossman
illustrated by Sylvia Long

Chronicle Books • San Francisco

One lonely traveler riding on the plain.

Two graceful dancers asking for some rain.

Three busy messengers sending out the news.

Four clever trackers looking for some clues.

Five wise storytellers trying to keep warm.

Six nimble runners fleeing from a storm.

Seven merry mischief-makers playing hide-and-seek.

Eight patient anglers fishing in a creek.

Nine festive drummers beating on a drum.

Ten sleepy weavers knowing day is done.

SIOUX

1 The Plains tribes depended on buffalo for food, clothing, bedding, and housing materials. They followed the herds, moving camp when the buffalo moved to new grazing areas. Prior to acquiring the horse, these tribes used dog travois to carry wood, food, small children, and the elderly. Although the child in this illustration is pictured alone, she would actually be part of a large group traveling together.

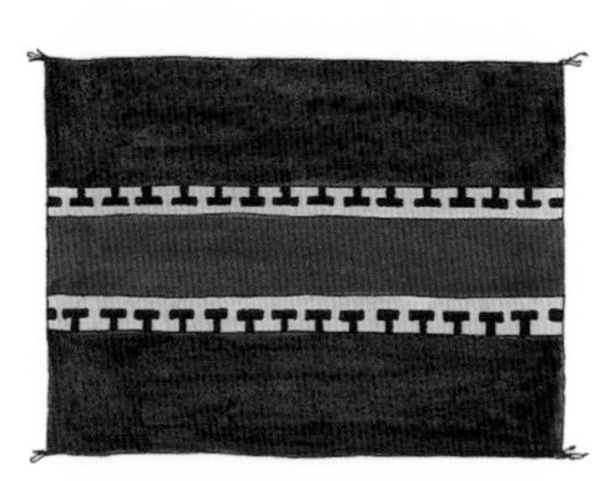

TEWA

2 Traditionally, all Rio Grande pueblos stage a corn dance, generally in the Spring. The dancers wear crimson parrot feathers and cowrie shells from the Pacific and carry gourd rattles. The male dancers leap and stamp to wake up the spirits. Finally, their evergreen finery (symbolic of the fir tree that, according to legend, people used to climb up from the underworld) is thrown in the river in the hope of pleasing the *Shiwana,* the rain-cloud people.

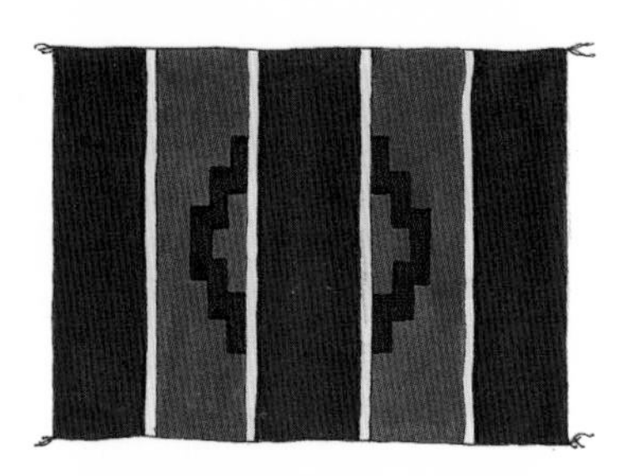

UTE

3 Plains tribes used smoke signals as a method of long-distance communication. Using a system of short and long puffs, they sent messages about such things as the presence of buffalo or the approach of enemies.

MENOMINEE

4 In the Great Lakes region, hunting bear had both practical and symbolic importance. Its fur was used for warmth, its flesh for food, and its fat was used as cooking oil, medicinal salves, and insect repellent. Its claws often made prize ornaments.

BLACKFOOT

5 Storytellers have always been a respected part of traditional Native American culture. They carried with them the legends, myths, and personal history of the tribe. In the oral tradition, this history had to be passed from one generation to the other by word of mouth.

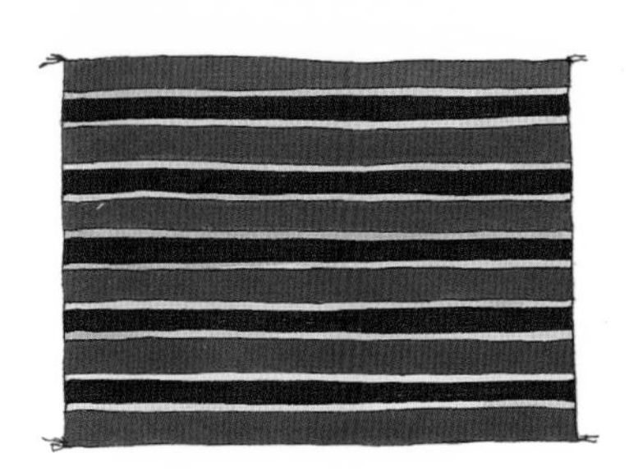

HOPI

6 The Hopi lived on the tops of mesas in Southwestern areas that had no permanent watercourses. Because of this, they farmed in the desert below where the success of their crops was dependent on rainfall and flash floods.

ARAPAHO

7 Because tribes often had to be mobile in order to survive, it was essential that possessions be kept to a minimum. It seems likely, toys and games were not considered a necessity, and so children had to rely on simple games to entertain themselves. Though there is no actual documentation of children playing hide-and-seek, it is possible that such a universal game was indeed played by children, both for entertainment and as a way to improve tracking skills.

NEZ PERCE

8 Tribes in the Northwest had no agricultural tradition until the missionaries came. Salmon was a staple food and noted fishing holes were considered the common property of the tribe. They supplemented salmon with trout, sturgeon, deer, elk, and small game.

KWAKIUTL

9 The Northwest Coastal tribes carved decorations on wooden drums, boxes, house posts, partition screens, etc. The masks and costumes in this illustration are from the Kwakiutl tribe.

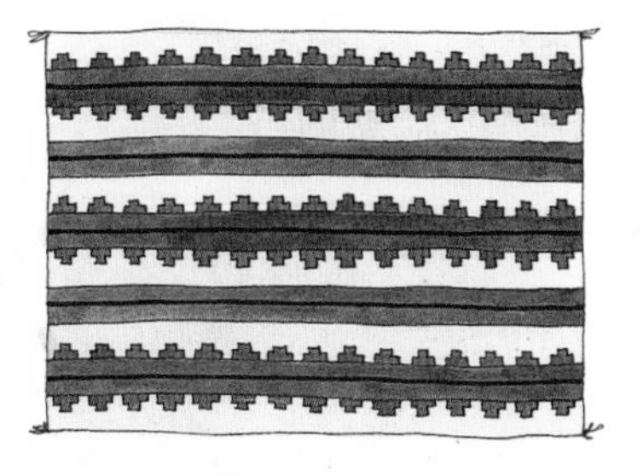

NAVAJO

10 For centuries, Navajo weavers have made beautiful rugs and blankets, both for their own use and for trade. It is said that the traditional patterns simply emerge from the weavers' memories and that there is always a break within the pattern so that the maker's spirit can escape.

DURHAM COUNTY LIBRARY
3 3450 00849 9160
ND
OCT 9 1
North Durham Branch Library
Riverview Shopping Center
5100 N. Roxboro Road
Durham, N.C. 27704
DISCARDED BY
DURHAM COUNTY LIBRARY